First One In: A Collection of Short Stories.

What goes through the mind of most people from day to day? I think you'd be surprised. Here are the thoughts of a few.

By

Eddie J Martin

Copyright © **2016 by Eddie J Martin**

All rights reserved.

Published in **the USA**

ISBN-978-0-9977521-0-6

No part of this book may be reproduced in any form unless written permission is granted from the author or publisher. No electronic reproductions, information storage, or retrieval systems may be used or applied to any part of this book without written permission.

Due to the variable conditions, materials, and individual skills, the publisher, author, editor, translator, transcriber, and/or designer disclaim any liability for loss or injury resulting from the use or interpretation of any information presented in this publication. No liability is assumed for damages resulting from the use of the information contained herein.

# Contents

If you're lucky, you'll remember all the good things that happen to

you in your life. If you're really lucky, you'll forget the bad.

– E


From *Enlisted at 14: Looking Back.*

Eddie J. Martin is a retired Air Force Sgt. who lives in Conroe, TX.
He is seventy-five years old and has been writing for four years.
This is his twenty-fourth novel.

To my daughter Beth, who has gone above and beyond my expectations. Love you.

Chapter one

Mama Said...

WE NEVER LISTEN, or we hardly do anyway.

Johnny, look before you cross that street. May, don't speak to strangers. Fred, there's snakes out there in that garden. Don't do this, don't do that. Used to drive me crazy.

When the old people tell you something, most times, they're right, so you better listen.

When I was growing up, my grandmother used to tell me that same thing, but did I listen? Most times, I didn't. Most times I got into trouble, I should have learned something, but I didn't. Maybe that's what brought me here, to the Ohio State Penitentiary.

I was only trying to make a few bucks. After all, my friends were all doing it. I liked Air Jordans too, but neither I nor my grandmother could afford them. My friends told me, "Just do this one thing, and you'll be able to get two pairs of Jordans. After all, Michel Jordan would want you to have them. So I did. One time, that's all it took. One time. I was to pick up the drugs and deliver them to X address, and I would get paid. One time, that's all I planned on doing. Just one time.

The cops followed me from the pickup location to the drop-off. They took twenty of us to jail that day, and it's said they confiscated over $50,000 in cash plus another $75,000 in drugs. Those Jordans were supposed to be my birthday present to myself – I had just turned eighteen that day. The judge felt it was his duty to try me as an adult and maybe teach me a lesson: "Don't want young men going down the same road as you. Maybe they'll listen to their grandparents." It didn't matter that my record was nothing like the guys I'd gotten arrested with. He felt I should get the same time.

I looked up at the judge, sad faced, and he looked down at me and shook his head. I could see he didn't want to do it, and the look I was giving him had worked before, but he gave me three years anyway – in the big house, no less. Never did get my Jordans. I'd stayed two months in the county jail waiting to see the judge, and now I was waiting to see where they were going to send me – upstate, somewhere close to home, I hoped so my grandma could visit me.

When I was in county, I had a chance to have some of the guy's school me about what it would be like upstate. The good news was that I was a big boy and they wouldn't try me so fast, but the bad news was that they would try me, try to take my shit, push me around, even make me their woman. "You can't wait until they feel comfortable doing this shit," one inmate said. "You have to start getting busy on their ass from the get-go. Whether you win or lose, you have to fight."

One of the guys told me a story about when he had first gotten up to the big house and they were going through indoctrination. He'd been talking to an inmate who had been there over thirty years already, and the inmate had told him the way it was up there. "First," my friend said, "the old-timer asked how many of us were there for one to three years. A number raise their hands. Then he asked who was there for three to ten years. A few more raise their hands. Then he asked who were lifers, with no possibility of getting out. More than one raised their hands.

"Then the old-timer said, 'Most of you have girlfriends. They'll be one of the first to leave you. Oh, they will hang around for a few months, some maybe for a year or more. Then the visits will be fewer, and then, letters, they'll stop altogether. I'm speaking mostly of the lifers, but somewhat with the short timers. The longer you are here, the more people you will lose. The first ones to cut you lose will be your friends; the last ones will be your parents. The one that stays with you the longest will be your mama, and eventually, she'll die off on you. So get ready for it; it won't be easy.'"

"Three years," my friend told me, "is not a long time, but then again, it may be. It all depends on how you work it." This was all going through my mind when, a few days later, the jailhouse bully stopped by my cell right after commissary on the day we get all our goodies. He demanded that I give him most of my stuff for protection. I didn't know what had come over this guy, because I'd thought we were cool. I was leaving soon anyway, so why was he starting this shit?

"I ain't giving you a God damn thing, so you can just get the fuck out of my cell," I said. He acted like he hadn't heard a word I'd said but continued saying, "I want this, that, and that."

"You can want in one hand and shit in the other," I told him, and I stood up and looked up at him face to face.

"Alright," he said, and he pointed his finger at me, shook it, turned around, and walked out of my cell.

Ten minutes later, three of his boys came into my cell and beat the living hell out of me. I woke up two weeks later in the infirmary with bandages covering my head and chest. *Well, I* thought, *so much for standing up for myself. If this is what's to come, I'm gonna have a hard three years.* Three weeks later, I was let out of the infirmary and taken back to my cell. My transfer time had come and gone, and my next was in three weeks. Commissary was in two.

The day of commissary, the bully came in my cell right on time. Earlier, I had collected my goods, and I was sorting them out.

"How you feel Ron?" he said. He walked into my cell. "Feeling better since the last time I saw you? I hope we don't have the same results this time. Got the goods all ready for me, I see. Now, let me see. I'll take that and that. As you can see, I brought my own bag."

I stood up, looked him in the eye, spit in his face, and said, "Fuck you."

He took his shirt sleeve and wiped his face and then took his finger and shook it at me. Then he turned around and was about to leave when I grabbed my sock out of the commissary bag, which had a steel golf ball inside, and swung it as hard as I could at the back of his head. He dropped to his knees like a sand bag, and I kept hitting him, head, back, and ribs. I closed the door to the cell, and it locked. I surely didn't want to be disturbed at this point.

The bully's men ran up to the cell door, trying to get in, but couldn't. The bully was lying on the floor, not moving but bleeding like two hogs while I continued wearing his ass out. The bully's men, seeing that they couldn't get in, started calling for the guards. Two minutes later, the guards got there, but the damage had been done.

Two days later, before I was taken to the hole, I got a chance to talk to my friend and thank him for the ball he'd given me and instructions on how to use it. He informed me that the bully would be out of business for six months or more; they believed he had brain damage. Other inmates were starting to attack the bully's men, thinking they could take over where he'd left off.

Thirty days later, they let me out the hole and sent me to the big house. I have no doubt now that I'll be able to do the three years, since now I know how to play the game. All of this could have been avoided if only I'd listened to what my mama had said.

Chapter two


Reunion


JANICE had her eyes closed when she felt someone kiss her on the cheek, and just before she was about to give the person a hi-ya, Jesse said, "Janice, I would have recognized those breasts anywhere. What the hell you doing here in Jamaica?"

"Jesse Bo-T, well, I'll be damned. Jesse, how long has it been? A couple of years at least."

"Janice, you still with the company?"

"Yeah, I'm still with the company, Jesse. What are you doing now, and have you seen Dorothy lately?"

Janice sat up and turned around for Jesse to tie her halter. "The last time I saw her, she was in Hawaii and had married this high roller about twice her age."

"Dorothy was near forty-three or forty-four herself. This guy must have been near dead."

"Yeah," Jesse said, "but knowing her, I'll bet she had a plan."

Janice put her arms around Jesse and said, "Jesse, it's sure good to see you again."

The guys who were walking by at the time Janice was hugging Jesse said, "Lucky mother jump."

Jesse was a player, and occasionally he ran drugs. He liked the ladies, and the ladies liked him. Five foot eight, one hundred seventy pounds, brown skin, black eyes, and curly black hair. Thin black mustache and a small cut on the corner of his mouth. A cute little guy, Janice had always thought. There was only one woman that she knew he was crazy about, really crazy about: Samantha!

"Are you working, Janice, or on vacation or what?"

"No, I'm on vacation, Jesse. Just out here chilling, as you can see. How about us getting together later for dinner, catch up on old times?"

"You got it, Janice. I got a little mama over here I was on my way to."

"You still running the ladies, Jesse? You never slowed down?"

"You know me, Janice. Where you staying?"

Jesse, Dorothy, and Janice had worked together some years back. She had gotten really close to them, but they hadn't wanted to stay with the company like she had. The company had gotten Dorothy out of prison after she'd served five years for killing her boyfriend's girlfriend. They'd been about to put Jesse in prison for going AWOL from the military and skipping out with the drugs and money of those he'd been working for. They—the feds—had made all of them an offer that they couldn't refuse.

They'd succeeded in closing out that case in record time, and three more after that. Jesse had never been too much into the job, but he'd done it, and they'd all gotten pardons after the jobs were done, all except Janice. They'd informed her in no uncertain terms that they would never let her go; she'd often wondered why.

It would be nice getting together with Jesse again. Janice knew he would have some stories to tell.

Meanwhile, in Hawaii, Dorothy's husband had died, and she was at the funeral. Many people were there, and she was glad when it was over. She knew few of the people there anyway. She and her husband had been married for less than two years, but long enough for Dorothy to convince him to change his will and leave everything to her, a little over $200 million. Now her retirement was assured.

They had, or he'd had, homes all over the place—Alaska, England, there in Hawaii, and one in Jamaica. They had just been in England six months ago and hunting in Alaska this past February. That was where he'd gotten pneumonia. So, to get away from all those headaches, she thought she'd go to Jamaica this time. All she had to do was contact her pilot, call the staff there, let them know she would be going, and go. Her lawyers would have to go there to finalize everything. They had mentioned something about double indemnity insurance; in that case, she would think about replacing her aircraft.

*It's settled then*, she thought. *Jamaica it is.*


A week later, in Agent Jenkins's office, Agent Stone was saying, "I don't know, sir, what we're going to do. Everyone seems to be tied up with Afghanistan and Iran and other commitments. I've never seen it this bad since 9/11. For this next assignment, we're going to need at least three agents."

"I know we promised Janice a long vacation, but it looks like we're not going to be able to honor that promise," Jenkins said. "Even if we recruit her for this one, she'll need help. Any ideas?"

"I've been thinking about it, sir; you remember that first assignment we sent her on? Well, there were two other people with her, a Dorothy Malone and Jesse Bo-T. They did a hell of a job on that one and just about closed the operation down completely. Besides that, there were three other assignments that they did well on also."

"We need that team back together again; do you think we can locate them?"

"Well, sir, we know where Janice is, and I'm sure she can find the others. She did it before. I'll get right on it, sir."

Al Ham Bra Club, Jamaica. Jesse and Janice were sitting at a table in the middle of the room. Janice was wearing a low-cut white evening gown with white pearls and earrings. Her hair was up in a bun with a diamond stickpin on top. The rings on her fingers were mostly diamonds, but there was one surrounded with pearls and a ruby in the middle. The last was a figure of Midas's head with rubies as eyes. There was also a duplicate of that figure on her backside that only certain people ever saw. Jesse had a tuxedo on and the bling.

The club was packed due to the show they had: Natalie Cole, Al Jarreau, and George Benson were headlining, accompanied by a band of national acclaim. The show went on without a hitch for two hours, and Jesse and Janice enjoyed themselves immensely. They laughed and cried and patted their feet to the music. When the show was over, they were spent and happy. The lights came on, and they ordered another drink.

Jesse nudged Janice and said, "Look there."

From across the room she came, wearing a black silk dress open at the sleeves, and three-inch high heels. She had diamond rings on her fingers and wore necklace, earrings, and watch to match. At five foot eleven—over six foot with the heels—with light skin, and long legs, it was Dorothy Malone coming their way and smiling.

At forty-four, Dorothy was a beautiful woman. She was dressed like she had a million bucks, and her posture was that of someone who had been in the military, which she had. She stood tall, proud, and in control of her destiny.

"Janice, Jesse," she said, after hugging and kissing them both. "This is really a surprise. Never thought I'd see you two again."

After trading niceties, they went quiet and just looked at one another, remembering the cases they had been on and how it had all begun.

"Are you still with the agency?" Dorothy asked Janice.

"You know I'm not going anyplace," Janice answered, "even if I wanted to."

"What about you, Jesse?"

"Oh, hell no. I need my freedom. The last time I was involved, well, you remember."

"Did you ever get together with Samantha?"

"Yes, and no. You know how she looked when we were on that first case and we rescued her? The most beautiful girl I had ever seen. Then, on that next case, when I was supposed to meet her again… Hell, that was the only reason I agreed to help out. After we closed the case, I waited for her down in the barrio just like Janice said. She was supposed to show up at around eleven or twelve p.m. within three nights. All kinds of people were coming up to my car, wine heads, prostitutes, panhandlers, and whatever. Glad I had my piece on me. Almost shot me a sucker.

"Anyway, on the last night, about twelve p.m., I was about to call it and chalk it up as a no-show when this bag lady came up to me and asked me for money. Now, this same woman had come up to me before. In fact, the last three nights about the same time. She was pushing a grocery cart, wearing a long, oversize coat, shoes that one would wear in the circus. Big, floppy hat with hair underneath and dreadlocks to her shoulders. By this time, I'm mad as hell about Samantha not showing up and this woman bugging me. So I gave her five bucks just to get her the hell out of my face, and then she started complaining about the amount I gave her. She thought it should have been more.

"At this time, I was about ready to really explode and told her she better get the hell out of my face when she says, 'Jesse, don't you recognize me? Have I changed that much?'

"I stopped right there and said, 'Recognize who?' I'm really looking at this bitch now. I raised up in my seat, stuck my head out the window, and said, 'Samantha?'"

"She was undercover?" Janice asked.

"Yes, she was undercover. Fooled the hell out of me, but once we got to my hotel room and she took a bath and removed all that bullshit… Samantha in the flesh. It was well worth the wait. All of it."

Then it was Dorothy's turn. She told of traveling around the Caribbean, meeting different men, and finally meeting one elderly man who took a liking to her and decided he wanted to marry her. Found out he was worth some $200 million, and he didn't push for a nuptial agreement, against his lawyer's advice, because he had no family and was in his eighties. He died, and now she had it all, but it was still not like when they'd all been together. It seemed like that was when she'd felt more alive. Maybe it had been the adrenaline. She didn't know, but she hadn't felt like that since.

Then it was Janice's turn. She told of the assignments since she had been with them, the assignments to the Swiss Alps, with stops in Korea and Texas. The meeting with the pimp "Smooth" in Alaska and him introducing her to a detective named Ruben Kane.

"All this for the agency?" Jesse asked.

"Yes, all that for the agency," Janice said.

"Hey, I tell you what: the show's over, so let's get out of here. I want you two to see my home."

"You have a home here in Jamaica?" Jesse asked.

"Sure do, and you won't believe it."

"Dorothy, with the kind of money you have, I know you wouldn't mind letting a brother borrow a few bucks."

"Name it, Jesse, and it's yours."

Outside the club, Dorothy's limo, driven by a fine-looking Jamaican female of twenty-two, picked them up. As the old friends sat themselves in the back, Dorothy offered them a drink from a small bar.

Janice's cell rang. Looking at the caller ID, she saw that it was Agent Stone.

"Janice," Stone said. "I'm sorry to bother you on your vacation, but we have a situation."

"How nice," Janice said.

"Do you think you could locate Dorothy and Jesse? You'll need them for this next assignment if they'll agree."

Janice looked at both Dorothy and Jesse, and they looked back at her and said, "What?"

Chapter three

# Thoughts of a Madman

## Drive away.

The little kid of three or four fell off his bike. I looked over toward him and saw no grown-ups were around and wondered where they were. There was another young kid of five coming up behind him, but the kid didn't stop, just rolled on by. The park had a walkway going around, and at that time of morning, very few people were out trying to beat the heat of the day.

From what I could see, the kid was having quite a time getting his bike back up – I had thoughts of going over to help him but thought better of it. People get very protective when it comes to their kids, even with the best of intentions. Animals do the same thing; they go into a killing mode when it comes to theirs. So I just sat there in my car and watched.

A short time later, a car drove by (the walkway was right near the road, across a small creek). Two women were in the car, and they stopped after seeing the boy. Without looking around, the one on the passenger side got out, hopped across the small creek, through the small bushes, and picked up the kid. She left the bike where it lay, put the kid in their car, and they drove off.

By this time, my hands had tightened on the steering wheel and my body had gone rigid. During the whole thing, I had just watched. I thought about calling out, but I didn't.

I thought about dialing 911, but I didn't.

All I did do was drive away.

Request

She walked up to the thirtyish-year-old man who was sitting at the outdoor café and asked if she could speak to him. She had been watching him for a while, and he just did something to her every time she looked at him. A tingling feeling came over from her heart down to her vagina. *One time*, she thought. *Just one time for a few hours.*

"Sit down," he said. "How can I help you?"

"This may be an unusual request, and – I don't know – you have every right to think I'm crazy, but I'm going to ask you anyway.

"You can't go wrong by asking, but I would have no idea what a beautiful young lady like you would want or need from me."

She sat down at his table, underneath the umbrella, looked at him very seriously, and said, "I want you to make love to me, to fuck me."

He sat back in his chair, looked at the her, and said to himself, *Hell yeah, I'll fuck you. Only have to ask me once.* Then he said. *Hold on a minute, just hold on. Why in the hell would she want me to screw her? After all, I'm not the best-looking guy around here or the youngest, so why me?* He didn't speak to her, though. He just looked at her with a question mark on his face.

She saw the look and said, "Let me explain. I saw you sitting over here and thought that I'd like to make love to you – men do it all the time, ask for sex, that is, so why not a woman? So what about it?"

"What's your name?" he said. "And how old are you?"

"That's not important," she said. I'm old enough, but if you think that'll be a deal breaker, I'll tell you what. It's like this: once the deed is done, we never have to see each other again. So will you screw me? Only take an hour or two of your time."

After a moment, she added, "You're not waiting for me to offer you money, are you?"

"Well, to tell you the truth I would feel more comfortable if you would. It would make me feel like I'm not being had."

"Well, that will never happen," she said. "Take the offer."

He was still hesitant, so she said, "I'll tell you what. We can go into the restroom and do the do, and if we like it, then we'll go find a room somewhere and do it right."

"Good looking, we don't have to do that. I have a small apartment a few blocks from here. We can go there," he said. "My car is right across the street. We can leave now. Why don't you go over to the car, and I'll be right there as soon as I pay the waitress."

The girl went across the street and stood by the red Toyota while he paid the waitress, gave her a tip, and proceeded across the street. At that moment, a milk truck came down the street at an excessive rate of speed. The driver was looking at his cell phone and did not see him, and he didn't notice the truck until the last second. It hit him, knocking him twenty yards to the other side of the street.

The girl had observed him paying the waitress, leaving her a tip, and walking across the street. She'd seen the truck hit him in the middle of the street, seen him fly through the air and land on a parked car twenty yards away. She watched the scene for a few minutes without any kind of feeling or emotion and then walked back across the street to the cafe and sat at the same table he and she had just left.

Before long, she spotted another gentleman and said out loud, "He's kind of cute."

She walked over to his table and said, "Excuse me, would you mind if I asked a request of you?"


## Day job

I saw this lady almost every day at the parks I went to. Always, she was alone. I saw her and would watch her, although she was not my age, sixty-eight, which meant I had over thirty years on her. That's what I thought at first. I'd guessed she was in her early twenties, Asian but American raised. You can tell the ones who have been here most of their lives or were born here. I recognized her from having done two tours of duty in the Air Force in Asia; it took me back.

At most of the parks I ended up in (there were twenty-one around the city), there she was between nine in the morning and twelve noon. Mostly, she was wearing what most people in the park wear: shorts, cotton blouse with no sleeves, tennis shoes with white socks, and no jewelry, nothing out the ordinary except she looked better than most in what she wore. Her shorts were a little extra short and tight, and I noticed that she wore no bra. Walkers and runners, real runners, always wear bras. When I passed her, we would always speak to each other, but that was it. At my age, I walk slowly, and she would always pass me, sometimes twice. This went on for weeks, but I was beginning to see and notice strange things happening with this lady, not just at one of the parks but at all of them – or the ones I went to anyway. The first thing I noticed was the lady being stopped by a new Buick while she was ahead of me. I thought the driver was asking for directions. They spoke for a few minutes; I had almost caught up to her.

She disengaged and continued on. In most of the parks, they have at least two restrooms, each being about halfway through the park. At the other end of the park, I noticed she turned in to the restroom. A minute later, that same Buick whose driver I'd seen her speaking to pulled into the parking lot, and the driver walked into that same restroom.

I walked past the restroom, and they were still in there together. Halfway around the park, I saw her come out. Two minutes after that, the man came out, returned to his vehicle, and drove off.

This happened twice more that morning with various vehicles. I stopped at a bench to rest a couple of times, but I did notice when she left around noon. She walked to the parking lot to a brown SUV, opened the back, and brought out a bottle of water. When she opened the back door, I noticed there were two children in the seats, hooked up and ready to go. She sat on the back tailgate until the water she was drinking was gone, closed the tailgate, and got in the vehicle and drove away.

This went on all during the school term. During the summer, I never saw her – until school started again in the fall.


## Ali's Choice


"Who the hell are you," demanded Ali, "and how did you get in my house at three o'clock in the morning?"

"Oh, I'm nobody," replied the other man, "just a person who's wanted to meet you for a long time."

"Well, you met me. Now let me get back to sleep."

"Don't be like that, champ. I always heard you were a straight-up guy."

"Okay, okay. You got ten minutes. Hey, I just noticed something; your mouth is not moving when you speak."

"It's a long story, but I came over here to talk to you."

"You probably know all about me, so why don't you tell me about yourself. How can you talk without opening your mouth, and how am I communicating with you without stumbling over my words?"

"You're asking a whole lot of questions. Well, let me start here. My name is John. I was befriended by an alien from a galaxy far, far away. He gave me certain powers. One of them is to speak to you telepathically."

"And how did you get here?" Ali asked.

"Believe it or not, I was transported here. I saw your picture in a local newspaper and thought that you were one of the people I'd like to see before I died. Let's just say you were on my bucket list."

"And how am I able to communicate with you with this disease I have?"

"Same way, telepathically. Words don't come out of your mouth, but when you think them, I can hear you. The difference is between your mind and when the words come out of your mouth. They don't. They bypass your mouth and go right to my mind. Once you get outside this Earth's atmosphere, your body would change to that of an ordinary person."

"You're putting me on. How could that happen?"

"There is something out there that affects the human body that is just not here on Earth."

"You mean if I were in space right now, I would be like a regular person?"

"That's right, but there's just one problem. To stay that way, you have to stay out there."

"And how long would I have to stay?"

"Till you die Ali, till you die."

"How about contacting my people? Would I be able to do that?"

"From time to time, depending on the Earth's rotation, but basically, you'll be on your own. You do understand, though, that you would be alone but with no kinds of illness at all. And you never get old."

"Never get old? What kind of place is that?"

"Its space, Ali. You've never seen or heard of a place like this. The scientists haven't even heard of a place like this. I could take you for a visit if you like."

"Let me get this straight. If I go to this place your talking about and decide to stay, I would no longer have this illness, shaking, and speech impediment? I would be just like anybody else? And if I did this, I would live out there forever? But I would be alone."

"Well, only until the people from Earth find a way to get up there, maybe another twenty years. And remember, the space shuttle is already there."

"They tell me I don't have long to live, and I'm okay with that. I think I'd rather be here on Earth, where I was born, and have friends than to be somewhere with no friends and alone. And to live forever – I don't think so. So, Mr. Spaceman, it was nice talking to you. Your ten minutes are up."

Crazy

There she goes, a full-figured woman. I don't know why more men don't want full-figured women. It seems like only small men are crazy about these big women.

That's weird: whenever you see a small man, he's with a big woman. Same thing with a large vehicle: a small man always has a large vehicle. Don't know what it is.

Myself, I like full-figured women, and small women, and midsize women, and all women in between. Hell, I've always loved women of all colors and nationalities. I especially love pregnant women. I think they're beautiful.

I look in the sales papers on Sundays and the clothing store articles, and I see the women there in whatever dress they're advertising and notice something's missing. They don't look right. Maybe it's me just getting older.

The women in their bikinis, bras, and panties just don't do it for me anymore. There was a time when I used to get hard as a rock just looking at them… but the full-figured ladies show more, a lot more.

Where's the beef? Maybe that's the question for them. They look like stick men or women. Big women are always trying to lose the good stuff, and the small men are always wishing they'd keep what they got.

I once wrote a book with a woman as my heroine. I never wanted a model type as my heroine. I always wanted a not-quite-full-figured woman, if that makes any sense. But that's the way I saw her in my mind, in my book. Maybe someone five foot eleven, thirty-nine-inch chest, twenty-five-inch waist, and maybe thirty-five to forty-inch hips. Now that's a full-figured woman to me.

I once had a full-size woman, have one now. As I remember, they always seem to be happier, but when I think about it (now check this out), I started out with a thin woman just like in the sales papers, and after many years of marriage, I ended up with a full-figured woman anyway. Go figure.

The Alpha and the Omega

Life begins when you leave your mother's womb; from there, it's all uphill.

Great!

First, there's kindergarten, grade school, high school… those teen years. And then crying to get to the point where you can get out there on your own. And then there are the relationships that come and go. Bills up the yin-yang, maybe a failed marriage or two in between. A few years stuck back with your parents. Later, your parents leave you, so now you can't go back there. Now you're pushing sixty and looking toward retirement, except you never saved enough for that time, and now your kids have come to live with you because of the hard times they're having. They not only come, but they're not alone: they bring their wife and kids with them.

I heard once that a kid can cost somewhere around $240,000 from birth till they leave home, supposedly at eighteen. But what if they put that off till age thirty? What then? Someone lied to me.

The kids today don't seem to think very much about their parents. The little bit I do have I was expecting to spend on myself, my retirement. No long trips for me. I always wanted to return to Africa, but the only place I'm able to go now is the park and the beach or anyplace within a tank of gas.

I feel as though I'm getting to the end of that line where I'll be leaving here, and you know what? It may not be that bad.

I've seen the good side of life, and I've seen the bad, the happy side and the loneliness. Love and hate, what more is there?

Diploma

I thought once about how many women I've made love to, how much time I have wasted copulating. When you think about it, a lot of time gets wasted just by screwing. I've tried figuring it out over time, say starting at age eighteen till thirty. Twelve years.

Copulating, let's say, three times a week, fifteen minutes a hit, that's forty-five minutes a week. I know, I know, a good man could probably do better than that, but I am only talking about an average guy.

Forty-five minutes a week equals 180 minutes per month,

equal three hours. Twelve times that equals thirty-six hours a year. One hundred and forty-four hours for twelve years. That's an associate's degree or better.

So you see what I'm saying; I could have gone a long way – in school, that is. But the thing about having sex is that, after, you're thinking not of school but of more sex.

When I think back, I could have had a PhD if only I had just cut back on the sex just a little bit.

So that's my fifteen-minute observation course and diploma if it were true.


Late night call

"Hello."

"Hello, may I help you?"

"Yes, and no."

"What do you mean, yes and no?"

"I just wanted someone to talk to."

"It's 12:30 in the morning. Why aren't you asleep?"

"I can't sleep. Besides, I've been contemplating committing suicide."

"Now, why would you want to do that? Doesn't anyone love you, or don't you love anyone? Why hurt them like that?"

"I don't know. I just don't seem to care anymore."

"Why are you talking to me?"

"Normally, when I call people they just hang up. And what

are you doing up this late?"

"Well, I wasn't up until you called. I was asleep."

"Are you married?"

"Yes, I'm married."

"Where is your husband?"

"He's right here beside me, asleep."

"I don't have anyone to be with. You're lucky."

"Don't give up. You'll find someone. You sound like a nice young fellow."

"Well, I'm okay, I guess. I just don't like being around a lot of people. I think something is wrong with me, and I don't know if I am straight or gay, whether I 'm coming or going. You ever feel that way?"

"I do, and you're not alone. A lot of people feel that way so stop fretting."

"Well, I think I talked to you long enough. I sure appreciate you talking to me."

"You're not going to do anything crazy are you? You sure would disappoint me if you did something like that."

"No, I'm good since I've talked to you. Thank you.


"Who was that?

"Oh, just some disillusioned young man who lost his way. Go back to sleep."

## Chapter 4

A Police Officer's Last Night

FIFTEEN MORE DAYS on the job, and I'll be out of here. I can't believe it's been close to thirty-five years. Thirty-five years of eating shit. Of giving out tickets, breaking up fights, car chases. Three car accidents, total of almost two years in the hospital and another two and a half in rehab. All that time and only four citations, one promotion, which was taken back because of cutbacks in the force. Desk duty for a year for on unintentional shooting. I thought the guy was going for a gun. Turned out to be just a cell phone. By the time I was aware of that, I had shot him. Didn't kill him, but he did go to the hospital. People need to be careful when reaching for anything when a policeman has a gun on you. Glad they didn't have cameras at that time. My ass would have been grass.

Right after they got those damn cameras, one of the guys got caught dragging a black guy out of his car for no reason. The camera not only caught the visual but also the vocal of what was said. Not even the policemen's union tried to help him after that. Quite a few of the guys had gone down since those cameras came into being. We thought it would help us, but just the opposite; it's bringing more of us down than it is them. It's been like this ever since Rodney King got his ass kicked by the L.A.P.D; that's when I first remember someone filming what happened. That was bad enough, and then came the riots. We've been catching hell from then on. Even now, you've got some officers who forget that the cameras are even there, and they still say or do something stupid. Facebook, Twitter,

YouTube, all this shit makes it so you can get it now in real time. In the old days, you could beat a guy's head in, and there would be nothing said, brother officers would look out for you.

Today, everyone is looking out for themselves; even with the force now, you have to watch your back. Just the other day, I started smacking on this black for sassing me, and my young partner jumped in and stop me. That would have never happened in the old days; he would have helped me. I once had on altercation with some folks on the road, almost had a shooting that time, and I was about to light them up when my sergeant pulled up. He eventually let them go on their way and gave me a lecture for stopping them. The sergeant. and I almost got into it right there; maybe that's why my promotions have come few and far between. After so long trying, I just decided to stay in this squad car, kind of be my own boss. I can tolerate the fights, robberies, etc.

The only thing I can't stand is domestic violence; now, that's the pits. Once, I went over to a home, and the man was beating up on his wife, and I tried to stop him, had to use my baton. The wife saw this and jumped on my back. I had no choice but to lay the baton on her head too. That was before the cameras. I got called in for that one too.

Not too long after that, I came upon almost the exact same thing except the woman was beating the husband with a broomstick handle. I looked at the situation, man on the floor holding his head and bleeding, the woman standing over him saying, "He just pisses me off!" All I said was, "Ma'am, I think you should get him a towel," and I left. Sometimes, it's best just to stay the hell out of it.

I had one partner get killed on me during a stakeout. We were backing up some detectives when the guy came out of the building firing a machine pistol. We were behind the police car door with him on the left and me on the right. The gunman's shots went straight through his door, three of them, killing him instantly. It took over fifty shots to take down the gunman. We found out later he had on an armored-plated suit. Sometimes, things go bad.

Stopping by the ladies of the night and getting a head job while on duty used to be no problem; everybody did it. Now they're all bitching, and I don't see any harm. Now there all talking about their rights. How the hell does a prostitute have rights? At the pay rate we're getting, they should be happy that we're getting extra benefits.

There was a time when we could stop a vehicle just for the hell of it. Now we need a court order to do anything. The respect we use to get, that's gone. I think that's directly to do with them damn cameras. Now, with the Internet, Facebook, Twitter, everything that happens in the country is live as soon as it happens. Seems like we have an incident happen to us three times a week. Everyone now has a phone, and on that phone is a camera, and on that camera is a video recording everything we do. Rodney King has come back to haunt us. They even have us wearing those damn things now, there in our vehicles, in the stores and in the streets. Wherever you go, whatever you do, now there is a camera. Wherever I go, I just assume there's a camera there.

There is more of my brothers in blue been convicted for one thing or the other than ever before, and I don't see anything changing. No one's backing us anymore. We get a new chief of police when the last one has been replaced, right or wrong. They still end up being on the civilians' side, covering their own asses. There is no one out there anymore to help us.

Justice, justice, everyone seems to want justice. God damn, we were giving justice; it's just everyone wants it. And, after all, we are the law, and whatever we call it, it's justice. So a few people get shot up; you have to expect that in a free society. I'll go home tonight to an empty house where a wife has left me and taken the kids. I've almost gotten to the point a few times of committing suicide. Some of my brothers have done just that because they couldn't handle it any longer, but I been holding off. My best friend right now is a bottle of vodka, many bottles of vodka.

Thirty-five years on the job, and I must admit I don't see anything but changes (and not for the better) happening now. Today, they are bringing in younger and younger officers and, some say, even smarter. We were all young once; I was a young cop once myself. Maybe the time has come to step aside.

There was one young man I met early in my career who was trying to get onto the police force, and he told me a story about why they wouldn't hire him. He was telling me about the Mexicans coming into the country. He said if he caught them that he would shoot them all in the head. So I said to him, "A lot of those people just come here to find work and feed their families." He said he didn't care; he'd shoot them in the head anyway. I asked him if he'd told the people downtown what he'd just told me. "Sure, I did," he said.

That happened over thirty years ago, and I never forgot it. That was a sure enough nut, but I guess some still got through.

I'll leave here tonight and go home to my wife (vodka); every night it's the same thing. I don't even feel good about having a beer with the fellows after work anymore. The talk is always the same: pulled a guy over, gave him a ticket because I didn't like the way he looked. One said, "I made a person get out of his car and walk the line just because I got tired of driving around alone." Another said, "I almost shot this black guy just because he was black, but I'm glad I didn't. I don't feel like writing all those reports."

I'm beginning to get more and more like that. I think it's the job. Night after night, I would hear things like that. I won't lie; I was right there with them once. I think I may take off now on sick leave. The calls I'm getting I'm not responding to anyway, due to the fact that anything might happen before shift ends.

Now they're starting to fire on us like we're the criminals. It used to not be that way. Now the uniform is a target and disrespected. What the hell is going on? It's like going to the jungle and hunting the animals, but now the animals are firing back. Now the chief wants us to get out of our vehicles and start walking, to get to know our communities better, he says. Travel in twos, make friends, make them like us. It'll never happen, and it's all bullshit.

Bad accident call, I'm not responding. Domestic violence call, I'm not going. Robbery of a convenience store, I'm busy.

It's time I get off; I have a wife to get home to. This last ride to the precinct sure feels different. Maybe that's the way it feels when you going through stuff for the last time. I remember once there were women I had sex with, and when I was leaving them, I knew; I just knew I'd never see them again. I felt the same way about my third wife. 'Bout like this job here, I know that I'll never be back, and I won't miss it, the guys, all the bullshit, none of it. From here on out, it'll be just me and my wife forever.

Going down one of the side streets in the direction of the precinct, most of the streetlights have been shot out, plus there's glass all in the streets. The streets are deserted. Two teens run out in front of me, and I have to brake hard to keep from hitting them. Both stop right in front of me, pull out long guns, and start firing into my vehicle. The last thing I see is the spider cracking in the window multiple times before my eyes close.

I never hear the sound of the gunfire or the windshield breaking. I never hear the young men saying, "Die, pig, die!" or them running away. I never feel the squad car ease to the side of the curve, stop and stay running. I have no flashbacks, like they say happens when you're dying, of kids, ex-wives, job, or friends; I have none of that. I never hear a thing. Everything just goes black.

## Chapter 5

### America, I'm Home

I walked across the boulevard, not thinking about the cars. I never paid any attention to them anyway; I just pushed my grocery cart with my worldly goods, and the only thing on my mind was getting to the other side without losing anything. I've made this trip many times over the twenty or so years since I left Vietnam. I've caught hell ever since I returned to the states and got out of the military. I couldn't get out of my uniform fast enough due to the civilians giving me so much hell: the names, spitting on me, calling me a baby killer, all that kind of stuff. My family couldn't understand what I was going through, so I started drinking more and more. Eventually, I had to get out of there, be on my own, around others of my kind.

It's been many years since I've seen any of my family, and we all stay in the same city. I doubt if they would recognize me now anyway. I haven't shaved or had a haircut in years, and my clothes are all from the alley and dumpsters. No, I'm not the man that they remember. I just don't like being around anyone, especially people who don't understand. Occasionally, I do run into a few of the guys from Nam, but they're all about like me, fucked up.

One of the guys said something about going down to the Veterans Administration, that they'd help me. I asked him, "Why didn't you go down? Have they done anything for you?"

He said, "Hell, no. They talk a good game, but they never come through. They did give me an appointment at one time for six months down the road. When I did go, they rescheduled me for another six months."

"So if they wouldn't help you, why you think they'll help me?"

"You may get lucky. They do give you lots of donuts and coffee while you're waiting."

They're always talking that **shit** about taking care of veterans, but that's just what it is, shit. You ever wonder about how, whenever there is a war, before going over, they have thousands of people out waving their flags. Yeah, they'll say, "Good old veterans, go get your asses shot off for freedom. We'll take care of you when you come back, trust us." How many people you see out there when we come back in body bags? Not many, I'll tell you that.

You got guys out here without a scratch on them, but they're as fucked up as the guys who lost limbs. I'm surprised that more of them haven't gone crazy on American society.

Sometimes, I think I should have followed the old boys to Canada, some 50,000 of them. Holed up there till the end of the war, come back, and continued my life as if I'd never left.

I believed all that rhetoric the government was saying about the world being overrun by Communists. Why should I have cared? There are places in my own country I can't go, but there I was like a lot of other Blacks, in the jungle, in the mud, ducking booby-traps and men shooting at me. Not to mention the mosquitoes, snakes, and other reptiles you would find in the jungle. The only good thing was the marijuana growing wild out there. Most of us stayed high most of the time we were out there.

Once, there was a rather large snake that slithered in one side of my foxhole. I was so high that all I did was watch him come in one side, cross my legs, and go out the other side. One of the guys saw the snake come out of my foxhole and said, "Hey, didn't you see that snake come out of your foxhole? Why didn't you kill it?" I told the guy, "That snake wasn't fucking with me. He just wanted a way out the hole. He wasn't out to kill me like others around here."

There are others who came back who had looks on their faces that they kept for a long time. The eyes, that's what I remember, the eyes. Those dead eyes. And not smiling. They'd had experiences that they'd only talk to another veteran about. I'm like that myself today.

I remember when I was in Nam, the Vietcong wanted to know what a Black man was doing over there anyway. "You got a war at home," they said. "You Blacks are crazy as hell. Here we are killing the whites while the whites kill the Blacks in the U.S., and the U.S. government sends the Blacks over here to kill us. It doesn't get any crazier than that."

Mohammed Ali was right when he refused to be inducted into the military and said, "Those people haven't done a thing to me, so why should I go over there and fight them," or words to that effect. And the ones that did go are steadily getting the shaft.

If you notice, they have female veterans out here also, not as many, but they're here. Where I might rip off an item or two, they do the same and sell their bodies besides. That's fucked up!

I sometimes create a sign saying, "Veteran. Need help." I make a few bucks that way, but I can only stand in one place for so long. Normally, people don't see me unless I have a sign or something, even when I'm pushing my cart, but the cops always seem to see me, especially when they want to take someone to jail. Every so often, they come after us because the higher-ups feel we're in someone's way. They never felt that way when they were sending us to fight. We are homeless but not stupid. A lot of us have college degrees, but because of the way we dress and our situation, if they think that they be wrong. It's just that a lot of us have problems, and we can't get any help from our government, the same ones who put us here.

This is how many of my days start: I wake up from off my park bench or in the alley, or from inside a doorway. Sometimes, I can get a little lean-to down by the river, but I have to watch my cart too closely when I'm there. I've also tied my cart to my big toe to keep from losing it. From the bench or whatever, I push my cart down to the Salvation Army for breakfast. After breakfast, I walk around looking through dumpsters, seeing what I can find. Once, I found a half-pint of Jim Beam whiskey. Sometimes, I find sneakers – I can always use them – plus clothes of all types. All these go into my cart.

After my search, I often stop by the liquor store and purchase a small bottle of wine. Then I find me an alley, sit down, and enjoy. Occasionally, another homeless person comes by, and I share with him or her; sometimes, but not always.

Sometimes, people see me and just stop and give me money. Their conscience is bothering them, I guess, or maybe it's the military hat and coat I have on. Who knows? Sometimes, the same people give over and over again.

Now, the winters are very different, except for my cart being difficult to push, but it's always there. I received a heavy coat and hat from the Salvation Army, and people will come out into the street when they know it will be around 0° and give out blankets, socks, sometimes coats, and try to get us into shelter for the night to keep from freezing. Some go and some don't. I don't, because I can't take my cart. I find a cardboard box on those particular nights, and I stay there.

Thirty-five years, that's how long it took for them to see us, to recognize that we are here. We've been here since we got back from Vietnam. Now, after all this time, you want to do something for us. Most of us are dead now; you do recognize that, don't you? A good portion of us are in prison, because no one thought to even imagine we might be sick due to our tour in Vietnam, the war that no one wanted except the politicians.

The suicides, the alcoholism, drugs, street life, loss of family, and loss of dignity. Now, after thirty-five years, they say, "We've got your back. Welcome home veteran." We've heard that all before.

Maybe they're being so nice to us now because we're into

longer wars, sending the same ones to fight over and over again. That means more disabled veterans, and more disabled veterans mean more money spent for their upkeep, a lot of money. Regardless of how much money they have to spend, they just have to spend it. The little money that they're giving us now, the homes and the medication, thirty-five years later, and some would say, "Paid in full." We would say, "Bullshit." Oh well, better late than never.

Now there is a new batch of veterans to lie to, and as always, I have no doubt that they will "do their thing."

Chapter 6

Dumas

White!

Now, she was white. She even wore a white dress, large floppy white hat, and white shoes. She also had red hair, green eyes, white teeth, and no jewelry, but she was white. When they talked about white people, they were talking about her. Nice shape, though, and cute. At about five foot four, she looked more like an albino than a white person.

When she walked into my office, I was sitting at my desk with a glass of vodka in my hand. After seeing her, I drank it all down in one gulp. She startled me that damn bad.

"Mr. Dumas," she said. "The investigator?"

"That's me, ma'am, and how may I be of service?"

"My name is Mrs. Stella Stone. I need your help on a very personal and serious matter."

"You came to the right place, Mrs. Stone. May I ask who referred you to me?"

"Good, Mr. Dumas. It's like this. I happened to be passing your building and saw your sign outside, and it said you were a private investigator. Are you private, Mr. Dumas?"

"I am that, Mrs. Stone; now, how can I help you?"

"When I walked in, Mr. Dumas, I didn't notice a secretary."

"No, ma'am. I'm a one-man operation. What you see is what you get. Now, how can I help you?"

"I believe my husband is trying to kill me."

"You want to explain that to me?"

"Well, for the last three months, I've been having to go to the emergency room. A few times, I passed out. The doctor, at first, couldn't find out what was wrong with me. Then, this last time after being tested, he called me into his office and told me that I was being poisoned, and then he asked who would want to poison me. I didn't answer him. 'I think you should call in the police,' he said. I told him I'd handle it, which brings me here to you."

"What would you have me do, Mrs. Stone? Find out if he's trying to kill you, how he's doing it? Why he's trying to kill you?"

"I've got the why, Mr. Dumas. He found another woman, number one, and number two, he's after the money. And one other thing, Mr. Dumas."

"Call me Dumas, Mrs. Stone. Everyone calls me Dumas."

"And you can call me Stella," she said.

"You were saying, Stella?"

"My husband thinks I'm too white."

"I don't understand, Stella; why would that be a reason to kill you? He is white himself, isn't he?"

"I think that I embarrass him, but I can't understand it myself. Our friends are all white, and they're mostly my friends, and it's all my money. There was a time when he loved me."

Before Stella left, I told her my rates ($500 up front plus $100 a day plus expenses) and told her I'd get right on it.

The info I got from her was that they lived in the higher-class section of town, 1021 Beacon Heights, near the country club and golf course – you know the type of area I'm speaking of.

I'd asked her, "How did you happen to find my place? After all, it is off the beaten path. She'd answered that after getting the news from the doctor, she'd just started walking and ended up on my street and seen my sign. Well, good for me. I need the work.

Her husband's name was Richard. He was five foot ten, 205 pounds, forty-two years old, and worked as general manager at a solar panel company. What I was able to find out about him was that he was a fairly good guy and everyone seemed to like him. He was having an extramarital affair, and there was one other thing: he liked to gamble, and he was in debt to some very unscrupulous people. Stella was worth a cool $5 million, so there you are: kill the wife, get the money and the woman, a scheme as old as time. When most people in his position would go to lunch from one to three… he would meet up with his woman at the hotel and have a little afternoon delight.

I also followed him to a hardware store and noticed him purchase a can of antifreeze. He didn't look like a person who would service his own vehicle, and if he was, it seemed to me that you'd need more than one can to do it. So there's the how.

A week after that, I informed Stella of what I'd found, including the name of the woman, where she lived, employment, pictures, etc. She took all the information, paid me my money, thanked me, and left. Wasn't bad for a week's work; now I could pay the rent.

A week later, Stella called me and said she needed to talk to me and maybe offer me a proposition. She would come to my office the next day at two.

She was right on time, this time wearing a black dress with black hat and high heel shoes. She also wore a black pearl necklace and at least three rings the same color. Stunning, that's all I can say. Absolutely stunning!

She came in with a walk like a tigress and sat down in one of the chairs in front of my desk and crossed her legs.

"Let me get right down to it, Dumas. My husband tried to poison me again, twice more, but while he wasn't looking, I poured the drink out. I no longer eat or drink at home. I can't live like that. And then, one night while he was out "working late," I came up with this idea, the proposition I wanted to talk to you about.

"My husband has been trying to kill me for three months now, that I know of. I know he'll continue trying unless I do something about it. So I came up with this… why not kill him first? I just need someone to do it for me, and that's where you come in."

It didn't shock me that much. I'd heard it all before; after all, I'd been in this business close to ten years.

So I looked at her and said, "Have you thought about just walking away? After all, you wouldn't be losing anything. You already have the money.""

"I don't know if you understand about how a woman thinks. I don't want to leave him, and I don't want the other woman to have him, and I don't want to die. I have thought about killing her, but he'd just find someone else. No, I think killing him is the answer. Now, will you take the job? I am prepared to pay you $100,000. Twenty-five thousand up front and the remainder after the job is done."

"Stella, that's a lot to take in. How did you know to even ask me something like that?"

"I've checked you out, Dumas. You're single, no kids, down on your luck, and willing to do just about anything for a dollar, and you don't care where it comes from or how you make it. I think that I'm asking the right person."

"And if I agree to your proposition, when would you want this job done?"

"Say, within the next two weeks. Surely before he gets to me."

"Let me think about it, Stella. Give me a day or two, and I'll get back to you."

"Don't take too long, Dumas. It's my life we're talking about."

I watched her getting into a white Jaguar from my window. It fit her very well: white on white in white.

One hundred grand, that was a lot of money, enough to set me up for the next couple of years. If I kept my wits about me, maybe longer than that. While helping myself, I would be doing a good deed and helping Stella also. Getting caught, there was always a chance of that, but I was a trained P.I.; I wasn't supposed to be thinking about getting caught.

Now, say I was to agree to her proposition; what would be the best way to carry it out? I could just outright shoot the guy, but that might lead the police right back to me. What about having it done? That meant more people would know about what was going on, and besides, that meant I would have to split the money with others.

My best bet would be an accident, I thought. Everyone had accidents. I called Stella the next day and said it would be a go as soon as she brought over the first installment.

I had devised an idea of how I was going to do it, and it would be a vehicle accident, a hit and run.

I knew that Richard and his girl went to an out-of-the-way motel and the same room, number 27. Two hours, they were in and out.

It took me almost two weeks before, one day, they went into the room carrying some kind of a bottle. This was a first; they must have been celebrating something. This time, they didn't come out until six. Regardless, I waited. When they did come out, I could tell they were both a little tipsy. At his car, they stopped and started kissing, caution to the wind. That was when I pulled out and got as much speed as I could and hit both of them, tearing off the door of his car at the same time. He was caught underneath my vehicle, and she was knocked inside his. I got stuck, with him underneath my vehicle, so I had to back up to disengage him. After doing that, I ran over him again and got the hell out of there.

The next day, in the paper, the hit and run was there, but it said nothing about a death, only that a woman had a broken leg and arm. The man had numerous broken bones and was in a coma, but he was alive. They had no idea who'd hit them.

*Well*, I thought, *I sure screwed that one up, and there goes my $75,000 out the door unless I get another shot at him.*

A week later, Stella came to my office carrying a small bag. She sat down and began telling me about her husband.

Before she started, I said to her, "I know you're disappointed, but as soon as he gets out of the hospital, I'll give it another try."

"No, no, Dumas, it's not like that – here." And she handed me the bag. I looked in it and found it was loaded with cash.

"There is $75,000 there, just what we agreed upon."

"But," I said, "that was on condition that I fulfill the contract."

"Dumas, you did better than that, Richard is paralyzed from the waist down. As far as sex is concerned, he can't do a damn thing, but now he needs me. There is nothing he can do for the other woman so she's out of it, and I do still love him.

"I'll get someone to take care of him, but from now on, he'll be right there where I can find him, and now I don't have to worry about him trying to kill me. I think now he'll be worrying about me leaving him."

"What about you, Stella? If he's an invalid, what good is he to you?"

"Sex, you mean? We weren't doing that much when he was home. Don't worry about me, Dumas. I'll be fine. I'll just do what you men do; I'll order out." She got up to leave and said. "You do good work, Dumas. I'll be sure to refer you to any and all of my friends who might be in need of your kind of service.

"Goodbye, Mr. Dumas."

Chapter 7


Dumas - Part 2


Frederick Dumas


is a different kind of private investigator. At thirty-two years old, he's been around the block. He's five foot eleven, 190 pounds, Black, with black eyes and hair and a tattoo of his old gang on his upper right arm. He's always wearing a straw fedora on his head in his hometown of Miami, Florida.

Up to the age of eighteen, he was the vice president of the Khalifs street gang. Then he enlisted in the Army for six years, was discharge, and started working with a private investigator, as his understudy. Once his employer was killed, he took over the business – after finding and taking out his mentor's killers. Dumas found out early on that following the rules hardly ever works, so he hardly ever plays by the rules. Whatever works! Dumas is willing to do whatever for his clients… up to and including murder.

The letter read:

>Mr. Dumas, that was a great job you did for us; we will be sure to refer you to all of our friends. This letter accompanies a check, a little more than we agreed upon. I hope this is to your satisfaction.
>
>Thanks again,
>
>EJ Morris, Ron Association

Nice, now this was nice. This would surely take me out of the hole. Mrs. Stone had been true to her word; she'd referred me to some top dogs with big money.

I'd done a job for her that had to do with her husband wanting to kill her, and I'd stepped in and stopped it. Of course, after that, she'd hired me to kill him, but I'd missed, and he'd ended up partially paralyzed. It had worked out for her, and she'd given me a healthy bonus besides.

The Ron Association was a billion-dollar company. They called me and mentioned Mrs. Stone's name and said she'd referred them. If possible, they wanted to set up an appointment with me.

Tuesday afternoon, at two p.m., I was at the Ron Association office of EJ Morris, CEO of the company. Mr. Morris was a typical businessman of fifty-five, wearing a three-piece suit, with gray hair, half-bald. He had a squared-looking face, a pot belly hanging over his belt and off a 300-pound body. He wore a Rolex watch and diamond rings, and he got right down to business.

They had an ex-employee who'd left and taken the company's secrets with him. If it was too late to retrieve the secrets, then they wanted to make sure it never happened again by sending out a message. They wanted the employee dealt with either way. "Use your discretion as to how you go about doing it," Mr. Morris said.

We discussed the employee and where he might be found or not. "If he sold the secrets," I said, "he probably won't be working anywhere in the area. He may even have left the country."

"Wherever he is, Mr. Dumas, we want you to find him."

We discussed my fees, $500 up front plus $100 a day plus expenses. "We will double that, Mr. Dumas; that's how badly we want this person. And Mr. Dumas, if, for some reason, he happens to die after you find him, just send us proof of his death."

Jamaal Wilcox, age thirty-eight, single, five foot eight, white, 150 pounds. He looked like a geek, but very smart. He had been working for the company for nine years, passed over for promotion three times. That, they thought, was the reason for the theft. Jamaal loved collecting travel books but had never gone anyplace, saying he couldn't afford it.

I asked Mr. Morris, "Why he was never promoted?"

He replied, "Wilcox was one of those guys who did his work, quiet, always came to work on time and never complained. To tell the truth, Mr. Dumas, he was just overlooked."

"How much you figure he got for those secrets?" I asked.

"Millions, he got millions."

First stop was Wilcox's apartment, a one-bedroom with a bath, kitchen, and living room. The usual furniture: couch, lounge chair with table. A few pictures of mostly scenes of foreign places: Jamaica, Finland, Iceland, Germany, and Australia. Travel books of the same. No particular book of one area. No family photos, and his bedroom and bath closets were absent of most of his personal stuff. Other than that, the place was clean. I checked with his landlord, who said that he didn't know that Wilcox was gone, that he was paid up till the end of the month.

His neighbor said that Wilcox was a very quiet person. The neighbor did speak to Wilcox every now and then, but Wilcox had said nothing about leaving town. When he did speak to the neighbor, it was always about traveling, mostly to Europe.

The travel books were mostly from one place, Rodman Travel Agency.

When I called there, I asked if they'd had a J. Wilcox traveling to Europe in the last couple of weeks? They had no listing for a J. Wilcox. He wouldn't be traveling under his own name anyway, so I asked, "How many people travelled during that time?" I was informed that there were seventy-five, and then I described him. The person I was talking to said she didn't know him, but there was one other person that worked there and she'd let me talk to her. The person I talked to next remembered him because he was traveling alone; most people going to where he went had someone with them. They usually go in a package deal. The other thing is that he wanted to get out as quickly as he could. "He's traveling by the name Reginald Armstrong," she said.

I thanked her and booked the same package that Wilcox had

taken.

I called Mr. Morris and informed him that Wilcox had left for Europe and that I was headed that way. I would call him when I had something. The package Wilcox had taken was to Germany, Amsterdam, Paris. I took that same package.

Our first stop was Berlin, and we stayed a night and a day there sightseeing. I found out that Wilcox or someone named Armstrong had stayed with the group all the time, and then I boarded the plane for the next stop, Cologne. There, it was a two-night stay of sightseeing and dinner at the hotel. I learned that there had been one afternoon when the group had been let loose on their own, but no one had an idea as to where Wilcox had gone. Their next stop was Mannheim, a spot not too far from Paris. Same arrangements, except when it had been time to leave, Wilcox had been a no-show.

Since Wilcox was a no-show at that location, I thought I would be also. I started searching around the city bus station and train station, checking my notes I had taken about him: his likes and dislikes, travel books that he looked at the most, etc. At the Bonn-Hof, I checked the schedules, and there was a town I saw that was in one of the travel books he had: Bonn Haven. It was a town of 2500, and it would be an eight-hour trip. Next stop for me would be Bonn Haven. The train was a typical European train, clean, fast, and on time. Eight hours later, I was stepping off the train in Bonn Haven.

I had a photo of Wilcox, so I began showing it around. Because of the language, it was rather hard, but I managed. Because the town was so small, I hit pay dirt rather quickly. At the third and last hotel I went to, they remembered him. They informed me that he'd stayed there three days and then left for, they thought,

Switzerland.

"How do you know it was Switzerland," I asked?

"Because," the clerk said, "I overheard him ask the bellhop how far Switzerland was from here."

Checking my notes, I noticed there were more references to the Swiss Alps then anyplace else, so I hopped on a train for Switzerland. It would take two days or more, depending on the snow.

My compartment held two women besides myself, one about twenty or twenty-one years of age, and the other one I guessed to be twenty-two. Both were your typical European women, blond, blue-eyed, five foot four, with the bodies of twenty-year-old's. They carried a picnic basket that held bread, cheese, and wine. After small talk, they invited me to dive into the basket. By this time, one of the women was sitting beside me, and the other was across from us. One of her feet was stretched out and rubbing my leg.

At around eleven that night, we were all quite tipsy, and it looked like the girl across from us was out. I tried to make myself as comfortable as possible, and then I felt a hand on my crouch. At first, I thought it was my imagination, and then, when I felt my zipper being pulled down and felt a hand grabbing my tool, pulling it out, and something warm engulfing me full throttle, I knew it wasn't my imagination. I looked down and saw the girl who was sitting next to me doing an oil well in Texas justice.

The next day, while the train had stopped, the girls got off to purchase more wine, bread, and cheese. I walked around, showing Wilcox's picture to see if I was still on the right track. There was a paper boy outside the station, and he said that he remembered Wilcox because he'd bought one copy of every paper the boy had, and he'd had five of different countries. Wilcox had given him a large note, but he'd had no change, so Wilcox told him to keep it. "It was a very large tip," he said. So I gave him a tip, just not so large.

Later, the girls and I were back at it; this time, they had three bottles of wine. Eleven thirty that night, one of the girls left the compartment and went to the bathroom. The girl who'd been sitting across from me the night before got up, pulled up her skirt, pulled down her panties, and then reached for my zipper, unzipped it, and pulled out my tool. She stroked it until it was hard (which wasn't hard to do) and sat down on top of it. ten minutes later, the other girl came back from the bathroom, saw what the other was doing, and said, "Gretchen, you said that you were going to wait for me!"

"I know what I said, but I just couldn't wait any longer." All the while, Gretchen was moving up and down, faster and faster. "Hold on," she said. "I'll be finished in a…"

She never finished what she was saying, but she came all over me. Before I could come, Gretchen fell off me to the floor. I was still sitting there, tool standing at attention and throbbing. The other girl saw all this and pushed Gretchen out the way, got down on her knees, and grabbed me by my tool in a lip lock. She wasted no time in giving me the release that I didn't get with Gretchen and that I deeply needed. After she was finished, the old tool was laid out like a limp noodle, and I knew I was done for the night. I normally need two hours to regroup, but I can actually say that I was done for the night.

But then Freda (the other girl) did something that made me respond in a way that I didn't think I was capable of: she grabbed my balls and pinched a nerve or something, and the next thing I knew, my tool was erect again. She jumped on board, and we were off to the races again. You learn something new every day.

During one phase of the trip, we got snowbound for two days, two more days with Freda and Gretchen. I really couldn't complain one bit.

On the fifth day, I made it to my destination, said my goodbyes to the girls with regret, and continued on my search for Wilcox, a.k.a. Armstrong.

I really hadn't dressed for this kind of weather. What I was wearing was okay for Florida, but it wasn't worth a damn here. I made it to the local clothing store, where I must have paid close to $2500 for what I purchased. Clothing wasn't cheap in Switzerland. I made sure I kept my receipts; the association wouldn't believe what I'd paid for this shit. I bagged my Florida clothes; after all, I did plan on going back.

The little village wasn't large, but it was spread out. There were no cars to rent, so I had to do the taxi thing. I did my thing with the picture and description, and as always with my luck, the last one I came to remembered him, and he had checked out a week ago. It seemed like I was about a week behind him, but I didn't see myself getting any closer. I was told that he'd hired a guide who'd taken him over the mountains to St. Moritz. So how in the hell would I follow him there?

"Do you ski?" he asked.

It so happened that I did. I hadn't always been a Florida native. I had to spend more money for the skis, and I keep those reccipts also. Once I purchased the skis and backpack, and found a guide, damn if a storm didn't hit. The guide informed me that we had to stay put until it blew over. I told him that I would pay double if we could leave right then. "No way," he said. "You don't want to be caught in the mountains during a storm." So we waited; three days we waited. As it was dying down, the guide felt that pass would be clear. It was okay to leave.

Once we got up into the mountains, I understood what the guide was concerned about. The Swiss Alps is a bitch. The Matterhorn really looked huge; throw in a storm, and you would have something on your hands.

Wilcox had to know how to ski to come this way, with or without a guide. "There is only one or two ways your friend could have come," said the guide. "This is one of them. If they left a week ago, there is no chance they got caught in the storm, but they did have to stay overnight in the mountains."

Wilcox traveled through the pass that the guide told him would be the longer way around to Zürich, but Wilcox said, "Regardless, that's the way I want to go. They stayed two nights at the grand Regina, a five-star hotel, on the way. After the mountains, which he was not accustomed to, he needed the rest. Anyplace that was inside with a bath. There was a place on the trail that was an area with a bed in it but no enclosure. He had read about such a place, but he couldn't see it being of any use to anyone other than lying down for a few minutes; you'd still be out in the elements.

*For some reason,* he thought, *these scenes look better in a travel voucher. I think I've seen enough of the Swiss Alps, although this apartment I'm in is outstanding: fireplace, bar, couch, and La-Z-Boy. Big-screen TV and king-size bed. This'll do for a couple of days, but I have to move on. No telling who the association has out looking for me. I'm hoping the trail I'm taking will hold them off, I'll travel around for about a year before I settle down in the area I've set my sights on.*

*All they had to do was give me a small promotion and raise like everyone else. I would have been happy with that. Even the women were making more than me, doing the same job. So why not steal from them? The secrets I took weren't the only ones they had; they had others. After all, they are a billion-dollar company, and I only received ten million for what I took. I probably could have gotten more, but I'm not a greedy man.*

Wilcox informed his guide that he didn't need him anymore. He wasn't putting on another pair of skis. He bought a ticket on the train for Zürich.

Three days back and moving fast (well, as fast as a pair of skis can take you and as much as the mountains will let you) I was right behind him.

At one overnight spot where we had turned in for the night, when the fire had died down, we were attacked by some kind of a large cat. The guide had his hunting rifle but couldn't get to it. All I had was my hunting knife that I'd purchased with my backpack and that I wore at my side. The cat was attacking my guide, so without much of a thought, I pulled out my knife and attacked the cat. I dived on its back, arm around its neck, and started stabbing it wherever I could. He then turned his attention towards me, swiped at me a few times, and limped away.

The guide wasn't hurt that bad because he'd been in his sleeping bag, but he did need some stitching up, and that's where we lost another day.

Two days later, we were at the hotel Wilcox had stayed. I learned that he had left three days before. We ran into Wilcox's guide, who was heading back, and he told us that Wilcox was headed for Zürich by train. So I jumped on a train for Zürich, 125 miles away. All I needed was for him to stand still for just a minute.

No Freda or Gretchen on this trip, but the scenery was out of this world. Of course, the snow was still a problem, and an eight-hour trip turned into a day and a half.

I had left my skis and backpack with my guide; the knife I'd kept. Since buying a pistol was near impossible in European countries, I'd decided I'd off Wilcox with the knife. I kept the box that it came in, deciding that if and when I had to declare it, it would be a gift.

Zürich was a fairly large city. Where to start? Since he had all that money and was not likely to get lost, I started at one of the best hotels in town, showing his picture there. I stopped at the cab stand outside the train station, but no one remembered him. After about ten hotels and three days, I thought of something. The cab drivers had a schedule. The train I was on had been supposed to get in at midnight, but because of the snow, it had gotten in at two that afternoon. Now, what if the cab drivers had two shifts, one day and one night. So I went back to the station late that night and began asking around. One of the drivers remembered him.

The driver said he'd taken Wilcox to a small hotel on the

outskirts of town. Wilcox had said that he wanted someplace quiet so he could write, that he was an author.

I asked the driver if he could take me to that same hotel. He said that he could but that Wilcox wouldn't be there.

"Why do you think that?" I said.

"Because," he said. "I picked him up three days later at midnight and took him to the airport."

"Damn," I said. What gate did you drop him off at?"

"The gate for Sydney, Australia."

I phoned Mr. Morris and told him of my progress up to then and that I would be heading to Australia.

"He's sure getting around, isn't he, Mr. Dumas?"

"Well, he's got the cash to do it."

"Keep me informed."

I purchased a ticket to Sydney, first class of course.

Somewhere over the Indian Ocean, the cabin started getting smoke in it, and the plane started going down, and the passengers were going crazy. I was one.

The ones who weren't belted in were on the ceiling, and the others were holding on for dear life. One lady was down on the floor, half in and half out of her seatbelt, asking for help and looking at me. I turned my head in the other direction; hell, I've got my own problems. I never did like flying, but sometimes, to get from A to Z in a hurry, you have to do it. Somehow, the pilot straightened the plane out so that when it came time to hit the water, it did so as though it was a regular landing, except it was on water.

I have to give it to the stewardesses; they were doing their thing, telling everyone about how to get out, how to use the flotation devices, and most of all, not to panic. Too late; I'd been in a panic ever since I'd seen the smoke. Everyone has their own fears about flying; one of mine is going down, and the other is going down in water, going in the water and meeting up with a shark and being eaten alive. Hey, that's just me. The pilot, I must say, had landed that plane, and not too many people were hurt. one hundred and fifty passengers on the plane, and everyone got out and into life rafts. On the horizon, we could see ships headed our way, and crafts begin circling around us. The ships eventually picked us up, and they gave us warm blankets and brandy. Damnedest thing, though: that plane never sank. It was still there when we lost sight of it eight hours later.

Two days later, Wilcox was in Melbourne, Australia, after taking another plane from Sydney. He was reading the local paper about the plane going down on the way to Sydney. *I was on the same flight a few days earlier*, he thought. Everyone aboard got off safely after being picked up by a cruise ship and were now all in Sydney. The aircraft was still floating in the ocean and it was being determined whether or not if it could be saved.

Wilcox had rented himself a villa outside Melbourne until he could figure out his next move. The villa had a housekeeper/cook and a yard man/chauffeur. The only place the chauffeur would take him was sightseeing and to the library. At night, Wilcox would sit on the porch in a rocking chair with a bottle of wine. He would always ask the cook for the local cuisine. He wanted to try everything new. He could wherever he went. *I could really get used to this*, he thought. Before he went to bed, he read a book about traveling, a glass of milk next to him.

Meanwhile, I was in my hotel room wondering how much more bad luck was coming my way. Two days on that cruise ship, although it had been nice, had put me back at least a week or two behind Wilcox.

Now, Sydney is a large city, and the cities Wilcox was visiting kept getting larger and larger. With ten million, he could have been anywhere. I went through my notes on the travel vouchers, Europe, the Swiss Alps, with Zürich being one of his main stops. It seemed like he'd gone straight through Zürich without stopping. Australia! Now, Australia is large; he'd come to Sydney for a reason. I was going to be needing a new pair of shoes for this; they were wearing out fast.

The boy was about eleven years old, and he came up to Wilcox's porch while he was sitting on the steps carving on a small piece of wood. When Wilcox looked up, he had to do a double take; half of the kid's face was screwed up, his left side, down to his mouth. His cleft lip was very apparent, and he lisped when he spoke. Wilcox stopped what he was doing because he didn't understand him the first time he spoke.

"Is my grandmother here?" he said.

"Who is your grandmother?" Wilcox asked.

"Mrs. Washington," he said, "the cook. I'm her grandson. I'm Ronnie."

Wilcox asked Mrs. Washington later about Ronnie's problems, and she said, "He's had that condition since birth. His mother died during childbirth, and I couldn't afford to get his condition corrected."

After his cook told him Ronnie's story, he told her he'd like to help. A week later, Ronnie left for the U.S., along with Wilcox's cook. He hated that, but Mrs. Washington had gotten him a replacement who was almost as good as her. He felt good about Ronnie and being able to help and look around for others he could help. After all, what good is money if you can't help someone? There was a school in Africa that needed school desks, children in need of food in Honduras, homeless in America. The list went on and on, and he tried to help them all, or at least the ones he could. But he figured a check here and a check there would help someone, and it would surely make him feel better.

He was at the Melbourne location for close to a month, and he felt that he should have been gone three weeks ago, but one gets lazy and wants a place to call home; he'd been lucky up to now. The association would never give up looking for him, though, so he made arrangements to move on.


I spent over three weeks in Sydney, and no trace of him. I needed to move on; maybe I'd have better luck at the next stop. I checked the map, thinking maybe he'd head for another large city to get lost in, but then again, there were hundreds of small places he could be, so then I thought maybe I should try there. That'd only take another ten years or so.

A few days later, after exhausting all my leads in Sydney, I decided on Melbourne; that was just as good a place as any. In the airport, a couple of hours before takeoff, I heard a person telling another that he'd just left the states, that his grandson was in the hospital getting cosmetic surgery. The boy had been deformed since birth.

"A stranger who was renting the house my wife was working at saw him and volunteered to help," said the man. "He paid for the whole thing, including sending my wife and me with him. I had to come back because of a death in the family."

After I heard that, I turned to the man and said, "I was listening to your story. That was a nice thing for someone to do. There are still good people in the world."

He agreed that there were.

"My cousin is like that, and I'm going to Melbourne looking for him, but I don't know where he's staying. This person you are talking about sounds like something he would do, but I don't know where he lives in Melbourne. Would you give me this person's address? Maybe he's the same guy."


As Wilcox was boarding the plane for Jamaica, Dumas was getting off his flight from Sydney. Wilcox had left a nice check for Mrs. Washington, and he had paid the current cook and chauffeur, called the rental people, canceled the villa, and was out of there for parts unknown.


I made sure I had my knife where I could get to it quick. I was sure this was my man after showing his photo to the passenger. This shouldn't take long, just verify it's him, do the job, take a couple of pictures with my cell phone, and send them back to Morris. My taxi pulled into the compound where Wilcox was staying. I knocked on the door, and his cook opened it. First, I asked for Wilcox. Then I asked for Armstrong, his alias.

"Oh," the cook said. "You just missed him by a couple of hours."

"When will he be coming back?" I asked.

"He won't be coming back; he's gone for good. We sure hated to see him go. He was a good man. He did a lot for the people in this area and others the short time he was here. If you ask the chauffeur, he should be able to tell you where he dropped him off."

I spoke to the driver, and he told me he dropped Mr. Armstrong off at the airport just two hours ago for a flight to Jamaica. "If you came in on that last flight from Sydney, you must have passed each other in the terminal."

God damn. So close and yet so far away.

"If you'd like to rent a nice villa," the chauffeur said, "this one is vacant."

I called Mr. Morris and told him where I was and that I'd missed Wilcox by only hours.

Morris said, "Damn if you're not getting closer. How soon do you think you'll have him?"

"With any luck, within the next week. With any luck."

"Stay at it, Dumas. I believe in you. And Dumas, thanks for keeping me up to date. Once this job is completed, I'll be able to rest well."

Jamaica! Now why in the hell would he pick that? A white guy would stick out like a sore thumb, even if it is a tourist location. But wherever he goes, I have to follow even if there is no other way but to fly. If I don't find him soon, Mr. Morris may pull me off the case and put someone else on it; it could happen. But he's traveling all over the map. Eventually he's going to want to settle down just like he did here in Melbourne. Then I'll have him.

Since it's not the money Morris is worried about, then I think it's about Wilcock making the association look like an ass. The big boys really don't like that. Well, like I told Mr. Morris, I should have his ass in a box soon.

From Melbourne, across the Indian Ocean to Madagascar, across the southern part of Africa to the South Atlantic, gas up in Brazil, and on to Jamaica. I should be collecting mileage for all the flying I'm doing, plus I've lost all track of time.


Meanwhile, Wilcock had rented a hut on the outskirts of town. Entering Jamaica, he'd had to go through customs, and he hadn't liked that. He had the best counterfeit passport money could buy, but there was always a chance that he could get filed up. *Technology is always coming up with something new. I'll have to watch that the next place I go.*

The hut was a one-bedroom with a family room and kitchenette. The back door led straight to the beach, and the front was a secluded road leading three miles away to the main road. He had rented a Jeep fashioned after the old World War II era.

*This should be good for a week or two, then I'll move. I'm near to where I wanted to call home, and I figure I'll be there soon.*

Three days later, I had made it to Jamaica, rented a hotel room, and was out at one of the local outdoor cafés having lunch, wondering where to start my search. Ten minutes into my lunch, I noticed an old Jeep coming down the road painted in rainbow colors. I was into vehicles like that, so I stopped eating to watch. The driver was a white guy wearing a straw fedora, a silk white shirt, and pants. As he got closer, I got a better look at him.

"Hot damn!" I said. "Wilcox! Wilcox. Well I'll be damned."

It was about time for my luck to change. Wilcox drove on past the café and stopped further down at an ice cream parlor. I got up from the table, placed a few bills down to cover the meal, and followed Wilcox down to the shop. When I got there, I watched Wilcox through the window; he was sitting at one of the small tables with a dish of ice cream.

Across the street was another café, and I got myself a beer and sat down to wait. Thirty minutes later, Wilcox came out of the shop, got into his Jeep, and was about to pull away when I jumped in beside him, placed my knife in his side, and told him to drive.


Two weeks later, Dumas had received the check Mr. Morris had promised him, but it wasn't quite as much as he thought it was going to be and he wanted to talk to Morris about it. Morris told him to come by his office the next day.

Morris may have been a little short on what they'd agreed on and what he'd promised to pay, but it had taken Dumas over a month to find Wilcox; he should have done it sooner. *I didn't get where I am today by giving someone more than they're worth,* thought

Morris. *I know what I said I was going to pay him, but money is money, and what would a nigger do with that kind of money anyway? When he comes by tomorrow, I'll stand firm and not give him another dime and dismiss him from my office. I like to face a person when I'm telling them to go fuck themselves.*

Ten thirty that night, at his home, Morris was sitting in his study with a glass of cognac in his hand and reading a book. I came in through the patio doors. I was in a black sweater, pants, and shoes. I was also wearing a black watch cap and black gloves, and had a pistol in my hand with a silencer on it.

"What are you doing here, Mr. Dumas? Our appointment is not till tomorrow morning. And why do you have that gun? Weren't you paid enough?"

"Yes, I was, Mr. Morris, and I'm not complaining, but I've gotten another offer, for your life."

Morris dropped his drink and told me, "Wait a minute. If it's more money you want, you got it. We can always negotiate. How much? Just tell me how much. Please, Dumas, don't kill me. I have too much to live for. I have a family. I have over $100 million in the bank. You can have as much of it as you want. I have too much to give…"

"Don't we all," I said. And I shot him between the eyes.

# Epilogue

After I had Wilcox drive back to his hut, I tied him up and thought about Melbourne and all the good things he had done. That shouldn't have happened, but don't let it be said I don't have a heart; but I did have a job to do and would be getting some good pay to do it. I sat down in front of him with the knife in my hand and just looked at him. It would be very easy to cut his throat where he lay, take a picture of him, and send it back to Morris.

"I knew you were looking for me. Mr. Morris send you?"

"Yeah!"

"I knew he'd never let me go. He never did like me because he thought I was stupid. He always made fun of me. It never was about the money. Did he pay you to bring me back or kill me?"

"Well, he doesn't want you back, only your photo showing you dead."

"How much is he paying you? I can do better if you release me."

"How much better?" I said.

"Five hundred thousand?"

I thought about that figure. I got up, and walked over to the bar, poured myself a large brandy, and took my time drinking it down. I walked back over to Wilcox and said, "A million. I want one million."

"I'll tell you what," Wilcox said. I'll give you two million if you take care of Mr. Morris for me. He'll never let me go even if you do."

"What do you mean by taking care of him?"

"Kill him," Wilcox said. "That's what he wants to do to me, isn't it?"

I thought about it and said, "We would have to stage your death until I can get back to the U.S. For now, I want you to transfer $1,000,005 to my account, and you can give me the rest after the job is done."

"You'll trust me for the rest?"

"Mr. Wilcox, I found you once; I can find you again."


End

## Chapter 8

## Hell on the Brain

When you think about hell, what do you think about? Someone saying that if you do this or do that you're going to hell? Some people have hell right here on earth; it's in their head, and they go there every day. The good things you don't mind remembering, and you go their time after time. But with those always come the bad, and that's where the hell comes in.

Remember the time you and your buddy were out on the town, and he got the girl, and you slept out in the car while he was up in the apartment making love? The next morning, early, he comes out, and for some reason, you thought you could ease up there and get you a little bit before she was fully awake. You tiptoed in the room while she was still asleep, took off all your cloths and got into bed. Then you put the covers over your head and made love to her. Naturally, she thought it was your buddy still in bed with her. You thought you could leave before she found out. But as you should have guessed, she did find out. She didn't raise no hell or anything like that, she just looked at you and said, "I told you last night I didn't want to make love to you," and that's all she said. All you could think about once you left there was, *Damn if I didn't get over*, until three days later when you came down with VD. Don't know if your buddy caught it or not; he never said. That's one of those things that happened that you keep to yourself, but it's with you constantly. You have no problems with the good things that happened to you, and you feel pretty good when you do think about them, but I'll be damned if with the good doesn't always come with the bad.

He was coming back from the village one night in Korea. Curfew was at twelve, midnight, and he was a little late by thirty minutes. If he tried to get in at that time, then he'd be written up, so he decided to cross over the fence father up from the gate. He picked a spot about 500 yards up and started to cross over. He felt that since there was a half-moon and every now and then the clouds would cover that, he had a very good chance of making it without being seen. He climbed the outer side of the fence with no problem (after all, he was an eighteen-year-old in damn good shape). At the top, he just put his leg over and started climbing down the other side. Don't know if this ever happened to you before, but halfway down, he felt something or someone was watching him, and he stopped right where he was. He looked left, and then he looked right. Nothing. And then something told him to look down. Looking up at him were three dogs, two German shepherds and one Doberman. The dogs never made a sound and never moved, just watched him. The shaking was almost uncontrollable, and he grabbed the fence so tight that he didn't want to let go, but after a minute or so, he managed to get control of himself. He started climbing back up the fence to the top, and then went over and down the other side. He looked back at the dogs, and they were still watching him, and they never made a sound. He walked down to the main gate and turned himself in. He felt he had dodged a bullet; nothing could have been worse than being torn apart by three vicious dogs. That's what happens when you try to enter a K-9 compound.

There are memories best left forgotten, but if only you could. There are always triggers that bring them back; they could be anything: a song, a word, someone who reminds you of someone you used to know, who reminds you of a situation you had at that time. It doesn't take much to trigger it, Then you're back there. Depending on what it was will determine the rest of your day, whether it's good or it's bad.

There are things you'd like to forget that happen to you in your lifetime; these are only a few of mine.

Chapter 9

Love lost

It wasn't always like this. There was a time when there was love all over the place. We couldn't make a move without hugs and kisses, couldn't keep our hands off each other. Where did it all go wrong? Over forty years of marriage, and now we can't stand each other. Today, I can't stand being in the same house with her. It's gotten that damn bad. Mad, mad all the time, about nothing that I can see. Arguments at the drop of a hat, but ten minutes later, she's fine. Tried touching her once, and I swear if she'd had a knife I would have been dead meat.

I tried to tell her that wasn't normal and that she should see a doctor about it. She does what she always does, told me I didn't know what I was talking about. It's been about ten or more years since I even hugged her, maybe longer since we kissed. If I want that, I have to go see my kids or to the park, I get more hugs and kisses in the park from strangers than I get at home. Sex, we're not talking about that. Every now and then, she wants to make love, but how do you make love to a woman without touching her? It ain't easy. The thing is, as far as everything else is concerned, she's fine. Cooking, she's always cooked. Cleaning, she's always cleaned. Some would call her a cleaning freak. It's not only with me, but with the kids also; they no longer come over, and if they do, it's only for a few minutes and there out of here. Smart kids. The only ones who seem to get a pass are the grandkids; she loves them. They get hugs and kisses. It's a whole different story when they're around; she even acts like we're a family. I believe that if you don't like something and you're not happy, you move on, and I told her so. I'd split everything we have down the middle. She could have her place, and I'd have mine. The bathrooms and living area she's always complaining about cleaning, because of me, I guess, she could just clean for herself. She wouldn't have to clean for me if we both had our own place. But she wouldn't take me up on it. It's not that bad now as long as I stay upstairs in my area and she stays down. I'm ready to move any time she is.

Today, all I want is to be left alone, to go to the park or to the library. I don't think that's too much to ask. Don't get me wrong; I'd like to walk in the park with my wife, holding hands and such. I see it all the time. People my age, sometimes with grandchildren, living out their days.

You're always hearing about the fortieth, fiftieth, or sixtieth anniversary of people my age, how much in love they were and have been for those years. How happy they have been. No one ever talks about the ones like me; it's like we don't exist. Is there a remedy for my situation? I have no idea. One thing I do know is you have to be happy, and if someone else is not happy, then you can't help that. It's a mental thing. If you let someone's unhappiness affect you; you will be as sick as them.

When did we stop loving each other? Maybe when we had the abortion. I felt we shouldn't have another kid; we had two already. She went ahead and had it (abortion) anyway, but naturally, down the road, she blamed me. Or maybe it was the kid by another woman I had before we got together. She never ever has forgotten that after all these years. Or it could have been a hundred other things that she's carrying around in her head that I am not aware of.

Life is very short, and if you go around with hate in your heart and always mad, you'll feel miserable, and no one will want to come around you. I'm happy for the ones who have been married all those years and love each other; it just hasn't happened to me.

End

# Chapter 10
## Purple Heart

I've never heard of someone say, "I've always wanted a Purple Heart," and I've been associated with the military for over fifty years. Everyone in the military knows what it takes to get one. The only way you get a Purple Heart is to be wounded in some way or the other, and then there is the ultimate: death. So no one in the military ever wishes for a Purple Heart, ever.

Although a lot of military people have them, they never wish for it. Some might even tell you they wish they never got it. I don't believe that's an overstatement. When you look at the service members that have been wounded, with lost limbs, PTSD, etc., all you have to do is go down to your local VA hospital, and you'll get a real understanding of how bad it is, and remember, all of these people have a Purple Heart.

Very few of the people who aren't veterans know about the families that it affects, the women who have to take care of their husbands, the kids who have to see their fathers in that condition, the pressure that's on them.

Then there are all the divorces, because some wives just can't handle it. Especially the ones who never had kids and their husbands came back impotent. All those guys got purple hearts.

The women who come back disfigured or with no limbs at all, veterans or not, society looks at them differently. As far as a future for marriage is concerned, it's slim to none.

All of these women have a Purple Heart.

I once read an article about a veteran who received a ticket for parking in a handicapped parking spot, even though he had the license plate and the disabled veterans card in the vehicle hanging from the rearview mirror. The cop saw him exit the vehicle, stopped him, and was about to give him a ticket (in fact, he did). The veteran tried to explain to him that all his paperwork was in order, so why was he stopping him? The cop replied by saying that he didn't "look like he was disabled."

The only way you can tell a person has PTSD, diabetes, blood pressure problems, or bone cancer is when they go off on you, but the Veteran's Administration has already tested you long before, and the results are all documented.

How do you feel about wanting a Purple Heart now?

## Chapter 11

## Back on the Block

When I think about the old gang, I have fond memories of some of the things that happened. Sometimes, I smile, and sometimes, I kind of hang my head in shame. There were many of us, and a lot of us were raised by single moms. That was one reason why a lot of us were out on the street. I was in a group call the Gaylord's, when gay was in a bad word. There was approximately twenty of us in the group, all living within a three- to six-block area. A few were like me, just hanging around because I had nowhere else to go, but there were none any younger than me. We all had sweaters the same colors, with "Gaylord's" on the back and our individual names on the front, on the left pocket. We had parties and went to movies, but we also got together to fight other groups.

No one really knew why we were fighting. We just did. I think if you asked someone today why we did it, they couldn't tell you.

One incident that stood out is what happened at the bar across the street from the barbershop where we hung out. One of the older guys had gotten into it somehow with one of the men in the bar. What I remember specifically is both being in the alley next to the bar, both standing apart from each other like in on old-fashioned western. Both had pistols in their hands as they faced each other. A few of us were standing across the street, watching. The young kid was in our group, but he much older than us and was known to have plenty of balls. All of us knew it; he would beat kids down with little or no hesitation.

Needless to say, the rest of us tried to stay on his good side. Lawrence had been in the reformatory a number of times and made it seem like if you'd never been there, then you hadn't arrived. A rite of passage, you might say.

The closest I ever got to that was a couple of cops getting a hold of me and changing my mind. The situation in the alley lasted a good twenty minutes. Lawrence never backed down, but there wasn't a shooting. The man went back in the bar, and Lawrence came back across the street. His reputation was already large, and it just got larger from there. Every now and then, I think about Lawrence as I do all the old gang, but if I had to guess about his well-being, I would say he's either in jail or dead.

Then there was Nikki, a very nice guy, preacher's son. He was a lot like me; the only difference was that he had a father and a mother. He hung around because he had to, 'bout like me. You had to belong to some group to live there in the area. If you didn't join one of the groups, then you had to be associated.

One of the larger groups I was going to join met at the schoolyard. To join, you had to fight one or more of the gang. When it became my turn, a number of police cars came around and broke us up. I really appreciated those cops for doing that, even though I never told anyone. The ones who didn't fight, we all told lies like: Why did those cops have to come around? I was more than ready to get down. We were told later that the group let us join without fighting.

There were guys like Lawrence who had understudies or younger kids who looked up to them, and those guys had aliases, like the person I was understudy to. His name was Jesse, and his alias was "Bull." Therefore, my name was "Little Bull." Now these guys all had three to four years on us, but we were in the same group (or gang). They were of all ages. Nine- to twelve-year-old's were called baby Khalifs, the thirteen- through sixteen-year-olds were called young Khalifs, and seventeen- through twenty-year old's were just call Khalifs. And then there were the much older men, in their twenties on up. These were the wine heads. At one point there, we had over 1000 kids, and a lot of them weren't nothing nice.

There was one day when I went outside and everyone was gone – I mean, the older guys, eighteen-and-up crowd. I don't know about the other guys, but I felt lost. After all, they were the ones who led the rest of us; they were the leaders. I found out later that all these guys had joined the military. After basic training, a lot of them came back wearing their uniforms, and they did look sharp. One thing I could tell right away: they all had changed. Just like before, I wanted to be part of it, but at my age, I knew there was no chance, but I tried anyway. Eventually, I succeeded in getting enlisted, and before long, I started liking it. I was still in a gang I figured, just larger.

Three to four meals a day, a cot, paid every month, and traveling all around the world, what's better than that? I think I'll stay.

Fifty years later, I look back and ask myself if I made the right decision. I think so. I get three retirements from other jobs, including the military, and all the medical care I need for life. I want for nothing. What more could a person ask for? But still, every now and then, I wonder about the old gang back on the block. Are they well, prosperous, with large families, or are they dead? After all, they did have three to four years on me.

Those thoughts never leave me; I guess they never will.

Chapter 12

Lost in time

A man can get lost in time, where he's back in a place that he loved at one time or the other, but I think that's what happens. Maybe that's why a person can look back and know if the time was good or bad and maybe want to go back there. I love living in the past, thinking about it. Oh, I know it's not reality, but things seem to have been much simpler then, much quieter then.

The people were nicer, the pace was slower, even the girls were not as quick to give it up then. Never thought I'd be saying that. The dresses were longer, not showing off as much ass as they do now, which is not a good thing all the time. The conversations were of an uplifting nature. I mean, if you left out race and all that it brings – let's forget that for a moment and just think how life was then. People talked to one another, you knew your neighbors, and parents looked out for each other's kids. In some cases, the neighbors would beat your kid's ass if they saw them doing something they shouldn't have.

Even the air just smelled better, the streets were cleaner, and the music was the best.

I think the best people back in the day were the grandmothers. They didn't take no shit, and they would put something on your ass if they caught you doing something wrong. But I never spoke to a person who doesn't love those old ladies to death right up to today. It's too bad the kids now don't have grandmothers like that; they just don't make them like that anymore. It seems like the old folks have passed away much too soon.

I used to have someone I could call and shoot the shit with, you know, family.

I mean, I've got my kids now, and their kids, but it's not the same. When my mother passed away – or it could have been my grandmother; I don't remember – one of my cousins said, "Now you're the grandpa." Well, I don't want to be no grandpa. I didn't elect to be the grandpa.

Now who do I go to for advice? Whose shoulder do I get to cry on when I'm down and out? Watching people die is the pits, especially when it comes to your own family. There is no hurt in the world like seeing your grandmother or mother die. I believe most of us leave here when our work is done, and I think we know when that time comes.

I remember when my grandmother's time came. Just before that, she started giving me stuff. One was an old pistol that her father had given her. It looked like something off the *Gun smoke* TV show. Another was an old antique train engine that she'd had for years and a couple of United States savings bonds. So I asked her why she was giving me all this stuff. She never answered me, but I figured it out later. We never had much of anything, and I felt that she was giving me what she had because I was not in her will. She had other grandkids, but I was the oldest. There was a pot (let's say), and she gave me a chance to pick from the pot before anyone else. I'll tell you, once she passed away, a lot of family members were looking for that stuff she gave me, but it was gone; and she made sure of that.

It was the same with my mother; she started buying me a few things and sending me her safety deposit box key and talking about her burial policy. She was telling me all this stuff, and it was going right over my head. I mean, this person had been there all of my life. There was no way she's going anywhere. But I'll be damned if they don't die and you're devastated, and you wonder to yourself why weren't you ready for this and how could this have happened when she was telling you all the time.

At a very young age, I enlisted in the military, and I remember that was during the time of Muhammed Ali, and he was whipping everyone who came along at that time. He was supposed to fight that day, and me and my buddy were in the day room, and we got us a seat in the back. During that time, they had only one TV, no larger than twenty inches, for fifty guys. There were very few of us (Blacks) there in 1958.

We knew Ali was going to beat this guy's ass, so we wanted to be in the back so we could gloat, and we weren't comfortable yet doing that at that time gloating in front of a bunch of white guys. When the fight began (and it didn't last long), Ali was beating the hell out of him, and we were going crazy. We couldn't help ourselves. The other fighter – his name was Harris, I believe – was from Texas, and the reason I mention that is because of the name of his hometown: Cut and Shoot, Texas. We laughed our asses off when we heard that. But today, the laugh is on me. Today, 2016, I live just ten miles from Cut and Shoot, Texas. Strange how things happen.

The one thing I could always depend on was my grandmother writing me while I was in the service, and when she did, especially on holidays, she would always put a dollar bill in the letter or card, sometimes two dollars. The grandmothers will be hard to replace, if ever.

I once saw a commercial about who was the law fifty years ago. They had a bunch of cops standing up, and then they had a group of grandmothers. And they asked the question, "Who is the law?" The grandmothers beat the cop's hands down.

## Chapter 13

## Some Women

Let's talk about women. I've known a few, quite a few really: Blacks, whites, Mexicans, Germans, Koreans, and Japanese. They are all the same, and yet they're not the same. There is one thing I found out that they all had in common: they all had high respect for the Black woman, and they didn't even know it. A lot of them didn't even have that kind of respect for themselves.

The questions I received the most were about Sapphire. I doubt if they ever even knew who the real Sapphire was. If you don't remember, then let me bring you up to date. Years back, they had a TV series called *Amos and Andy*. Kingfish was their friend, and his wife was named Sapphire. By the way, Amos and Andy, Kingfish, and Sapphire were all black. Kingfish was always getting into trouble, and Sapphire would be right there on his ass.

They didn't know the show, but they sure knew the name. I would hear all the time, "Do I look as good as Sapphire?"

"Can I dance as good as Sapphire?"

"Do I make love as well as Sapphire?"

Of course, my answer was always yes, yes, and yes.

It seems to me that there are a whole lot of single women out there who are looking to be taken advantage of or not, and if there were more of me, I'd sure help them out, but in my day, no one can say I didn't do my fair share. In my day, the fellows were just like me, but we've all gotten old now, and we were expecting to leave it to the youngsters, but there're not taking up the slack. They are not doing anything.

I'm seeing more gays now than I think I ever saw in my life. Therefore, if there is a man shortage with more gays coming out the closet, that means the men are getting securer and the women are getting more plentiful. Now, if a woman gets a man, she's holding on for dear life; she'll take a lot of shit before she'll leave. She'll take the abuse, the humiliation, the degradation. She'll take it all and say, "I'm staying with him because of the kids." Bullshit. That may have gone over the first time or even the second time, but the third and fourth and fifth time… I mean, what does it take?

I love women, even though they do get a little bitchy sometimes, a lot of times, really. When things get rough enough, it's time for somebody to hit the road. I've left a few times, and I've been left.

I've learned one thing doing all that leaving stuff: you must be prepared to lose. You are always going to lose something. My advice: don't worry about the material things… Just go.

If you are a woman, take your kids and go. If you are a man, get your favorite jeans and Jordans sneakers, six-pack of beer, and get your ass out of there.

I started this book wanting to talk about women. I've kind of gotten off track somewhat, but men get tricked into relationships to, although not as much as you women. And you probably don't hear about it as much, but the situation is out there. I've seen women literally beat the hell out of some men and humiliate others. I don't know what it is that makes an ordinary man turn into jelly when dealing with some women. Don't get me wrong; I know there are some strong women out there, and you may want to stay clear of them. I always did.

Once, I saw this incident outside a nightclub where this guy kept berating this woman and he wouldn't stop, so she let loose on him. Now, she was no small woman and built more like a tank than anything, so this guy had to be a little tipsy to go that way. By the time she got through knocking him upside the head with her fist, the guy hit the ground and rolled underneath a truck and wouldn't come out.

Now that was one bad woman!

And then there was Beverly:

Beverly had a nice family, a husband of five years and two kids, a boy and a girl, a house in the suburbs and two new cars. Her husband worked at an oil refinery company making better than average pay, and he worked long shifts, sometimes sixteen hours a day. Beverly was a stay-at-home mom; she'd get the kids off to school, clean up the house, go grocery shopping, and go to the gym for aerobics. The perfect life, you'd think, and it was for a while. Somewhere along the line, she started wanting more.

It might have been when she was having sex with her husband, John, and she started thinking about her aerobics teacher, or it might have been when the guy at the grocery store started giving her "that look." It could have been when that TV repairman came in the house right after she'd gotten out of the shower. That wouldn't have been so bad if she wouldn't have just stood there naked and without moving. He looked at her, and she looked at him. For at least ten seconds, it was that way. That's when she knew there was something wrong, and that was her first indiscretion. There were to be many more after that. Maybe she was doing that because John was her first love and they'd gotten married straight out of high school, and she'd never known anyone else, never wanted anyone else.

Then John started coming home with these porno movies. He said they would make their marriage even better than it was. Turns out he was right. She never expected that while he was at work, she would look at those films. After he went to work, she'd watch those films, and she found herself watching those films more and more. And naturally, after watching the films, you want sex yourself, and playing with yourself won't get it. She started going to the porno movies in the mall every morning after her husband went to work and the kids were off to school. You'd be surprised how many people are in there during the day, men and women.

Once, she was there sitting beside another woman, and in the middle of the movie, she felt a hand near her crouch. She had on a rather short skirt, and it had risen up to and above her thighs. The hand lay on her thigh at first and then moved up to her panties. It stayed there for a few minutes, and then the fingers moved her panties aside and entered her vaginal area. During the whole time the other woman was doing this, Beverly made not one objection, but she did think to herself, *I'm letting another woman do this to me. I would never...* But the movies and the sexual encountered had led her to this point. She climaxed that morning at least three times, and she made it a point to make it to that theater every Wednesday after that.

Her husband was getting weirder and weirder himself. After a while, he wanted to do the three-way thing, and it worked fine for a while until Beverly suggested that they add a male and replace the female, in fact, having a four-way. He wasn't for that at all. "I don't want to be classified as no punk," he said. Say what! And they never did it.

By this time, she was screwing everybody from the TV repairman to the lawnmower man, people she met in the park and the movies; she was just a slut. It came to her after she screwed the grocery store delivery boy, and believe it or not, she asked herself just what the hell was she doing. *Look at what I have and all that I have to lose. Up to now, things haven't gone south, but how long can that last? How long will it be before everything explodes, and then where will I be?* A week later, she spoke to John about her feelings, and to her surprise, he felt the same way and had been feeling that way for some time.

He said that he didn't say anything because he thought that was what she wanted, and he wanted to keep her happy. Sometime later, they took a two-week vacation to Hawaii to get started on their new track. Hopefully, they can stay on it.

Chapter 14

The Down Low

Ada wasn't no fool; she knew Otis was going somewhere other than where he said he was going, plus he'd been coming in lately now smelling differently. He'd leave her smelling one way and come back smelling entirely different. She knew his cologne, and what he came back wearing wasn't it. He smelled like some cheap hotel bath soap to her. She should know; she'd been in a few.

She thought she had found the perfect man, and they'd hit it off right from the start. He'd even told her that he loved her. You don't hear that too often from someone you just met, but what the hell, it was nice to hear. After a while, she started liking Otis more and more; I guess that's what happens in a relationship. Was this love? The sex was great; she couldn't ask for anything better.

Six months later, she met Wanda at the beauty parlor. Wanda's old man was a friend of Otis's. There were four of them always hanging out together. One thing led to another, and Wanda asked Ada to go over to the coffee shop next door with her.

While drinking their coffee, Wanda asked Ada if she had noticed anything different about Otis.

"Like what?" asked Ada.

"I can't put my finger on it. Like another woman but not another woman. You feel me?"

"Maybe it's another man," I said with a laugh.

Wanda wasn't laughing. "You know every Wednesday night the four of them get together and come back some eight hours later. He says they were playing poker, but there was something about his odor that told me something different. Not a funky smell that one would get after a poker game, but a lot sweeter, nothing from my home anyway. Have you noticed anything like that about Otis?"

"No, I haven't, but then again, I wasn't looking for it. But now that you mention it…"

Ada left Wanda, and she started thinking, *it wasn't my imagination. Most of the time that he came in, I was asleep.*

The next Wednesday, when Otis went out with the boys, Ada had a plan. She felt a little bit guilty.

He returned home at two that morning and went straight to bed. Ada was wide awake. She waited until she heard him snoring and crept over to where his clothes were on the chair. She picked up his pants and then his drawers and smelled them both. They smelled like a man but not the man lying beside her. She would know if it was another woman's smell, and that was no woman's smell. Ada took the drawers in the bathroom, turned on the light, and put smell with sight. Things really didn't look right at all. What was Otis into? She went back to bed, but she didn't go to sleep; she just lay there.

She called her brother the next day, told him her suspicions, and asked him for help. Henry was a street hustler who sold drugs, among other things, and knew everyone in town. Those he didn't know; he knew someone who did.

A few days later, Henry called her and told her that he had that information she wanted but that she wouldn't like it.

"Go ahead, Henry. Let me see if my suspicions are correct."

"Okay, Ada, here goes. It seems like your boy and the other three have an apartment over on Doucette Street. They get together on Wednesdays, but that's not the only time. They may be there anytime, just not altogether. No women are ever seen. I hate to tell you this, Ada, but I think your man is on the down low."

"What the hell is the down low?"

"Men screwing men. That plain enough for you?"

"No, Henry, tell me your lying!"

"I know the guy who owns the apartment building. I'm not lying. He says it's been going on for over a year. Ada, if I were you, I'd go get myself checked out."

"Thanks, Henry. I think I'll take your advice."

The doctor gave her a clean report, but she still called Wanda and told her what she'd found out. Wanda knew the other two girls, and Ada told her it was up to her whether or not she wanted to call them, that she was packing right then."

"Ada, come pick me up when you finish. I'm out of here too."

As Ada was putting her bags in her car, Otis drove up. "You going someplace?" he said.

"I know, Otis. I know it all. I could ask you how you could do this to me, but I have a feeling you were doing this long before I came along. Was I just your cover?"

"Something like that," he said. "I do love you, Ada. I really do."

Ada got into her car and, without hesitation, drove a way. She did take one last look back in the rear view mirror, one last look at her past.


End

## Epilogue

Have you ever been in love? Do you want to be again? I'm sorry to tell you this, but if you've been in love once before, you don't get a second chance. One is all you get, one real love; all the others, you'll be comparing them to the first one. The second, third, and all after that haven't got a chance. Oh, you'll get all the words, no worries about that, like "I've never loved anyone as much as I love you" or "You are the best lover I ever had." You don't say anything because you're saying the same thing too. The truth is, it'll never be the same as it was the first time. Never.

Forever gone is the way that you felt when you were around her, the way that you felt when you touched her, the way you could never keep your hands off her or her you. While in the bed together sleeping, she was right there underneath you. Where did it all go wrong?

I envy those who have it and pray for those who don't, and wish all the time that I had it all over again.

Other books by this author:

Enlisted at 14: A Memoir
Enlisted at 14: And the Journey Continues
Enlisted at 14: Looking Back
Willow: A Novel
Willow: One for the Team
Willow: And the Medusa
Little Miss Willow: A Short Story
Assassin
Blacker the Berry
Meet Ruben Kane
R.K. {Ruben Kane}
Ruben's Bag
Ruben's Bad Side
Smooth: A Ruben Kane Novel
Mo Kane
Here 'Tis
And Then Some
Dear Client Ducks in a Row
Just a Dream
Dream Catcher
Beyond the Curve
Switch

www.ingramcontent.com/pod-product-compliance
Lightning Source LLC
Chambersburg PA
CBHW041409010726
47507CB00001B/50